Stick your favorite picture here

A special message for you

Goodnight Sweet Mateo, child of mine,

Held in my arms you're safe and fine.

I gently place you in your bed.

Lay down your pretty sleepy head.

Mateo

You're small, and every day is long.

But sleep my love, and you'll grow strong.

I hope you have amazing dreams,

Of toys, and games, and yummy ice creams.

Goodnight Sweet Mateo, now go to sleep,

You need to rest, so please don't weep.

For a loving child I would always pray,

When you were born, it made my day.

Mateo

All of your family loves you so,

And that love just grows and grows.

You have so much fun ahead of you,
There's nothing that you cannot do.

So, snuggle up with your stuffed toys,

You have no worries, life is a joy.

Goodnight Sweet Mateo, close your eyes,

Don't worry about the hows and whys.

You'll make friends, and laugh and play,

To make the most of every day.

Time goes so fast, and soon you'll grow.

Love life my child, go with the flow.

Throughout your life I'll guide your way,
So from your goals you will not stray.

Goodnight Sweet Mateo, sleep my love,

I am always close, like a hand in a glove.

Mateo

Listen to all the advice I give,

I will teach you the secret of how to live.

Some days are good, and some days are bad,

But, I hope you are happy more than sad.

A soothing lullaby will help you rest,

For you I want the very best.

Goodnight Sweet Mateo, please hear my song,

Morning will come, it will not take long.

Goodnight
Mateo

Made in the USA
Las Vegas, NV
19 November 2023

81135181R00026